Friendly Faces

written by Sarah Albee
illustrated by Joe Mathieu

Contents

studio BOOKS

White Plains, New York • Montréal, Québec • Bath, United Kingdom

Can Elmo Take Your Order?

A hungry customer walked into a restaurant for lunch one day. After looking at the menu for a few moments, he knew what he wanted to eat.

"Good afternoon, sir!" said the waiter brightly. "Can Elmo take your order?"

"I would like a tuna sandwich, please," said the man.

"Elmo is very sorry, sir, but we are out of tuna sandwiches today," Elmo replied.

"Oh. I see," said the man. He studied the menu again. "In that case, I guess I'll have a grilled cheese sandwich, please."

Elmo shook his head, "We're out of that, too."

"All right. Can you bring me a salad?" asked the customer. "I'm very hungry and I'd like to eat!"

Elmo shook his head again.

"Well, what DO you have then?" asked the man.

"Elmo thought you would never ask! Today's special is . . . peanut butter and jelly, sir!"

"But, I don't want peanut butter and jelly!" exclaimed the man.

"Well, sir, peanut butter and jelly is the only thing the chef knows how to make."

7

The door to the kitchen suddenly swung open.

"Here comes the chef now!" said Elmo excitedly.

"Hello, everybodee!" yelled the chef, waving at all the people. "It is I, Grover, your cute and adorable chef, here to serve you!"

"You!!!?" gasped the man. "I should have known!"

"Congratulations, sir!" said Grover. "You are the 100th customer of the day! You win the grand prize!"

"What's the grand prize, Chef Grover?" asked Elmo.

"The grand prize is . . . one hundred peanut
butter and jelly sandwiches!" Grover said excitedly.
"Oh, you are so lucky!"

Everyone in the restaurant burst into applause.

"Why me . . .?" murmured the man wearily.

Zoe Helps Out

"Hi, Zoe!" called Big Bird. "Are you ready to go to Snuffy's birthday party?"

"I sure am, Big Bird!" replied Zoe excitedly. "I even remembered my present!"

"I'm bringing him this big bunch of balloons," Big Bird said.

"But I just realized I left his birthday card back at my nest. Can you hold these balloons while I run back and get it?"

"No problem, Big Bird!" said Zoe, taking the bunch from him.

As Big Bird hurried away, Zoe began to imagine.
"What if I could float away?" she wondered.
Suddenly, her feet felt lighter. She imagined she was
floating off the ground!

Zoe wondered what it would be like to float high up in the sky. "Whoa," she imagined. "I'd be really high up in the air." She decided it would be exciting. "Sesame Street sure would look different from way up there!" she thought.

She imagined drifting slowly along, looking down at the world below. "Everything looks so small from way up here!" she thought.

"But, how would I get back down?" Zoe wondered.

She imagined a little bird fluttered over to her balloons and landed on one of them. It popped one of the balloons with its pointy little beak.

With a huge feeling of relief, she imagined she was slowly drifting back toward the ground.

"Thanks for the help, little birdie!" Zoe called to the bird.

13

Zoe imagined landing lightly on the ground in the same place Big Bird had left her.

"Thanks for holding the balloons, Zoe!" said Big Bird, out of breath.

"No problem, Big Bird," giggled Zoe.

"Oh, dear!" Big Bird said as they began to walk away. "I forgot the cake! Can you hold these again while I run back and get it?"

Zoe looked at the balloons, then at Big Bird. "I think I've had enough excitement with these balloons, Big Bird," she said. "Why don't I run back and get the cake and *you* hold onto the balloons?"

Cookie Monster Can't Wait

"Cookies still not done yet?" wailed Cookie Monster. "Time spent waiting for chocolate chip cookies to bake seem like eternity!"

Big Bird sat down next to him. "You just put them in the oven, Cookie Monster," he said. "How can we keep your mind off the cookies while they're baking?"

Just then, the Count came walking by. "Hi, Count!" said Big Bird. "We're trying to think of something to do while Cookie Monster's cookies are baking. They still have twelve minutes left to go."

"Ah! Twelve!" said the Count. "Twelve minutes until the cookies are finished! Wonderful! That's 720 seconds! I will count them for you!"

17

A fire truck zoomed by, clanging its bells and blaring its siren. It pulled up right next to them and the firefighters jumped out of the truck to rescue a stranded painter. It was very exciting to see! But Cookie Monster was still thinking about cookies.

"That's one! One daring rescue! Oh, and there are 558 seconds left to go on the cookies!" said the Count.

Next a parade marched by. A juggler juggled four
balls, clowns cartwheeled, and bands *oom-pah-pahed.*

"That's one quick juggler, two cartwheeling clowns,
and three band members playing out of tune! *Ah! Ah! Ah!*
And 212 seconds left on the cookies!"

After the parade had passed, Big Bird sighed and shook his head. "I'm afraid I can't think of anything else to do to take your mind off those cookies, Cookie Monster," he said.

Suddenly, Cookie Monster sprang to his feet.

"Look at that little boy!" he exclaimed to Big Bird, pointing toward a little kid in a stroller. "What kind of food you think he is gobbling? You think he eating cereal? Or, maybe crackers? Or, or, or even grapes? Here! Wait for me, little boy! Want to share with your friend, Cookie Monster?"

"That's one! One distracted monster! *Ah! Ah! Ah!* And five seconds left on the cookies in the oven," said the Count.

Ding! "Hey, Cookie Monster, the timer just went off. Your cookies are done!" said Big Bird. "Where did you go?"

"Zero! Zero seconds left on the delicious chocolate chip cookies. *Ah! Ah! Ah!*" Count said excitedly. "It is time to eat. Then we can count the crumbs left over!"

"Me no need cookies anymore," answered Cookie Monster, his mouth full of pretzels. "Me sharing snack with little boy. Cookies yummy, but sharing with friend even better!"

That's two! Two happy friends! And nine cookies getting cold!